PROJECT
BEST FRIEND

MORE RULES FOR

PERFECTION

(ALMOST)!

Private List for Camp Success

PENELOPE PERFECT

PROJECT BEST FRIEND

Chrissie Perry

ALADDIN

NEW YORK LONDON TORONTO SYDNEY NEW DELHI

🪔 ALADDIN

An imprint of Simon & Schuster Children's Publishing Division
1230 Avenue of the Americas, New York, New York 10020
First Aladdin paperback edition April 2017
Text copyright © 2015 by Chrissie Perry
Interior illustrations copyright © 2015 by Hardie Grant Egmont
Interior series design copyright © 2015 by Hardie Grant Egmont
Cover illustration copyright © 2017 by Marta Kissi
Published by arrangement with Hardie Grant Egmont
Originally published in Australia in 2015 by Hardie Grant Egmont
Also available in an Aladdin hardcover edition.
All rights reserved, including the right of reproduction in whole or in part in any form.
ALADDIN and related logo are registered trademarks of Simon & Schuster, Inc.
For information about special discounts for bulk purchases, please contact Simon & Schuster Special Sales at 1-866-506-1949 or business@simonandschuster.com.
The Simon & Schuster Speakers Bureau can bring authors to your live event. For more information or to book an event contact the Simon & Schuster Speakers Bureau at 1-866-248-3049 or visit our website at www.simonspeakers.com.
Cover designed by Laura Lyn DiSiena
The text of this book was set in Aldine 401 BT Std.
Manufactured in the United States of America 0317 OFF
10 9 8 7 6 5 4 3 2 1
Library of Congress Control Number 2016931511
ISBN 978-1-4814-6602-8 (hc)
ISBN 978-1-4814-6601-1 (pbk)
ISBN 978-1-4814-6603-5 (eBook)

PROJECT BEST FRIEND

CHAPTER

Penelope Kingston wanted to be perfect. And most of the time she was good, sensible, and calm. But nobody is perfect. Sometimes Penelope was bossy, angry, and frustrated. It was like (and this is very weird) there were two Penelopes inside her. She was never sure which one was going to be stronger on any given day.

So even though she knew she wasn't perfect, Penelope tried hard to be excellent at most things. After all, excellence was very nearly perfection.

Penelope sat on her carefully made bed in her very neat bedroom. She liked everything to be just so. It made her feel a bit panicky when her room was messy.

She liked all her old teddy bears to be facing the same direction—toward the window, where she secretly thought they enjoyed the view. She liked her pens and pencils (sharpened, of course) to be nice and straight, points up, in her favorite mug.

Her books were currently organized by size, but last month she had arranged them by color. It all depended on her mood.

Once, Penelope had even arranged them from her most favorite to her least favorite. This had been quite difficult, though *When We Were Very Young* was absolutely and obviously number one and *Robot Spies* was absolutely and obviously last.

The rest of the house was usually too chaotic for Penelope's liking. Her bedroom was where she could feel calm and happy.

Penelope picked up her iPhone and cradled it in her hand. She loved her phone so much—more than she thought she probably should. She scrolled across to the camera function, chose video, and hit record, filming herself at arm's length.

"Hi!" she began, rather breathlessly. "I'm Penelope Kingston, and this is my bedroom!"

She reversed the focus of the camera and started to scan her room. She filmed the award certificates that were pinned up on her wall in perfect rows and then chose two to zoom in on. The first was a very special award called the Watchful Eye. Penelope had received it for taking good care of a kindergarten girl who had fallen over in the playground. Mr. Joseph had been on yard duty that day, but Penelope was the one who had spotted the emergency. She had taken the girl to the nurse's office and even stayed to keep checking her bandages way after the nurse had said she could leave (though unfortunately all that information was not written on Penelope's actual award).

The second was an award for punctuality—Penelope had a perfect record for being on time to class.

Every Friday at assembly, Penelope's school held an awards ceremony. Over the years, Penelope had earned thirty-six awards. (The next biggest award winner was Alison Cromwell, who had only twenty-one.) Of course, only some of the awards were on the wall. The rest were filed away in a special box with a lock and key, along with other important documents, like Penelope's birth certificate.

Penelope had decided that a video of her room would be the perfect introduction for the new girl. From the moment Ms. Pike had announced that a new girl would be joining their class that week—and that her name was Brittany O'Brien—Penelope just knew her life was about to change. Soon, everything would be perfect.

For starters, Brittany O'Brien was an *elegant* name, just like Penelope Kingston. Anyone with a name like Brittany O'Brien would most likely be aiming for excellence.

Second, it was absolutely time Penelope had a best friend. Everyone else in her class had one.

Whenever they had to get into pairs for activities or excursions, Penelope never knew who she would be paired with. And although she loved Ms. Pike, she knew that being partners with the teacher meant she was the odd one out.

PENELOPE IMAGINED HAVING TO PAIR UP, AND HER BEST FRIEND BEING RIGHT THERE NEXT TO HER.

She filmed her bookshelf, careful to show how neatly her books were ordered.

Next was the stand of jewelry she'd made, which Penelope sold at a booth she set up in front of her house each month.

Then she passed over a photo of her little

half sister, Sienna, wearing a tiara, absolutely the loveliest and most complicated piece of jewelry Penelope had ever created.

Giving away the tiara hadn't been easy, and sometimes (only very occasionally) Penelope felt a pang of regret about it. But Penelope's stepmother had told her Sienna loved it so much that she even tried to wear it to bed.

That definitely helped the pangs. Of course, the tiara was too pointy to wear to bed. (Penelope had tried, too. It had made a dent in her forehead that stayed there the whole morning.)

Penelope scanned over a row of earrings, making a mental note to give one pair to Brittany, absolutely for free, once they became best friends.

Next, Penelope zoomed in on a picture of a Gemini symbol, the twins.

PENELOPE THOUGHT IT MADE SENSE THAT HER STAR SIGN SYMBOL WAS OF TWINS. SOMETIMES SHE FELT LIKE TWO PENELOPES LIVED INSIDE OF HER.

Some days Penelope might think she was going to do one thing—say, be really kind to her brother—and then end up doing something entirely different, like shouting at him to leave her alone.

This would be an excellent thing to discuss with Brittany O'Brien, once they became best friends.

Just as Penelope pondered this, her phone buzzed with a text message. Careful not to look, she immediately covered the screen with her right hand and used her left thumb to stop the video recording.

She sat on her bed, her phone turned over so she couldn't cheat. Then she closed her eyes and ran through the possibilities. Who might have sent her a message?

It could be her mom, even though she was just downstairs. That had happened before, but it was normally when Penelope had her headphones on and couldn't hear her mom yelling up the stairs.

It was also possible it was her brother, Harry. Sometimes he would send Penelope a text ordering her to go to the candy store and buy him some lollipops. Penelope had never— not even once—obeyed him, but Harry was a slow learner.

Actually, there was almost no chance it was

Harry. Penelope could hear him playing on his computer—even though it was Sunday night, and Harry probably hadn't finished his homework or put his dirty clothes down the laundry chute. When he was playing World of Warcraft it took an absolute emergency to interrupt him. Perhaps a mass of *actual* assorted dragons flying though his bedroom window, breathing blazing fire down the back of Harry's hairy neck, would do it. Probably not.

It could be from her dad, but Sunday was his family day, so that was unlikely.

There were only two other people in the world who had Penelope's phone number. Alison Cromwell (the girl with twenty-one awards) was the only other kid Penelope knew who had her own phone. She doubted it was Alison, though. Penelope had sent her three different messages—once inviting her to meet in the library to compare awards and twice to suggest a playdate at Alison's house—and she hadn't received a single message back.

She was pretty sure Alison must have run out of minutes.

Penelope opened her eyes, keeping the phone face down. She even liked looking at the back of it.

Harry had an iPhone too, but his had been given to him just because he was starting high school. Penelope had *earned* hers.

Fifty-two percent of the money had come from her jewelry stall. The other forty-eight percent had come from her dad. Penelope sent him copies of all her school report cards, and he gave her twenty dollars for every A she got. She wished report cards came every week. Then she would be rich.

Penelope picked up the phone and held

it against her chest. Her best guess was that the message was from Grandpa George. She flipped it over. Her guess was correct.

> Hello, my girl. Your moon is currently in Venus. That means it's a good time to start a new project. It may take a while before the project bears fruit, but ultimately there should be a positive outcome. Keep your head held high and all will be revealed.
>
> G x

Penelope smiled. Grandpa's messages were long and sometimes a bit hard to understand, but this one truly did make sense.

Penelope could hardly wait for school tomorrow so she could get started on her latest project.

Project Best Friend.

CHAPTER

Penelope awoke to the soothing harp sounds of the alarm on her phone. She changed into her school dress and made her bed carefully, so there wasn't a single wrinkle.

She was just arranging two teddy bears on her pillow (side by side, but not quite touching) when Harry's alarm sounded in the next room. Penelope breathed deeply, trying to block out the motorbike sounds. This was an important day in her life. She was determined to stay good, sensible, and calm. Today had to be perfect.

Unfortunately, the kitchen was terribly messy, with all the dishes from last night's dinner still out on the counter. Penelope opened the fridge and sniffed the carton of milk. It didn't smell too bad, but she decided to play it safe, opting for whole-grain toast rather than cereal.

Penelope forced herself to pay no attention to Harry's alarm, which was still buzzing at regular intervals. Ignoring an alarm, even if it did sound more like a mosquito than a motorbike at this distance, was extremely difficult. But truly, Penelope had enough to do this morning preparing to meet Brittany O'Brien.

If Harry kept on pressing the snooze button, it *shouldn't* be her problem.

As she waited for her toast, Penelope sent her dad a screenshot of her schedule for the week. It hadn't changed much from last week, except that her Wednesday art lesson was being replaced by a music lesson. But Penelope liked her dad to have up-to-date details about her days. That way, when he thought about her, he would be able to picture her in the right place at the right time.

Penelope ate her toast, sitting on a barstool at the kitchen counter. She could see her reflection in the stainless-steel fridge. She tried to imagine she was seeing herself for the very first time. As though she were Brittany O'Brien.

She sat up very straight, trying to make herself look taller. Although her grandpa always said good things came in small packages, Penelope was very impatient to have a proper growth spurt. Sitting up straight definitely helped.

The girl in the reflection had a neat, dark brown bob. From the side, her nose was a little pointy, but from the front Penelope thought it looked rather nice.

Penelope made a mental note to face Brittany O'Brien front on.

After breakfast, Penelope packed her school lunch. She put in a whole-wheat roll with cheese, an apple, and a container of yogurt. She was pleased to see that (this time at least) her mom had bought everything she'd put on the shopping list.

As she fastened the clips on her lunch box, Penelope wondered about Brittany's height and hair and nose. It might be nice to have a tall friend. Then again, it would be lovely to have a friend her own size.

neat, blond shoulder-length hair ➤

slightly pointy nose, but only from the side ➤

almost exactly the same height as Penelope ➤

Brittany, Penelope's best friend!

PENELOPE IMAGINED WHAT HER NEW FRIEND MIGHT LOOK LIKE.

Then another muffled motorbike/mosquito noise broke into Penelope's thoughts, causing the image to fade. Penelope looked at the time on her phone. As annoying as Harry was sometimes, Penelope couldn't stand the thought of him being late to school again.

A few weeks earlier, Harry had received detention for being late and had missed an important soccer game. He'd been very upset.

Penelope could not resist for one more second. She charged up the stairs. Then she pinched her nose to manage the stink of smelly socks and opened Harry's bedroom door. Ignoring her brother's groans, she pulled the blanket right off him and put it over by the door. He'd have to get up to put it back on.

Next, Penelope went into her mom's room.

"Morning, Poss," Penelope's mom greeted her.

Her mom was sitting on the edge of her wrinkly, unmade bed, pulling on her shoes. There was a messy tangle just under the surface of her hair. Penelope found a brush under the jumble of things on her mom's dresser and pointed out the spot.

"Thanks, love," her mom said. She gave the spot just three strokes of the brush, even though Penelope was sure it would need at least seven or eight to untangle the knot properly.

When her mom stood up, Penelope noticed that her shirt (which was mauve, and quite pretty) was missing the second button from the bottom.

Penelope tried *extremely* hard not to mention the button. In fact, she struggled for thirty-two seconds. For the first seventeen seconds she reminded herself that she needed to get to school early. She was helping out with a sausage sizzle at lunchtime, and wouldn't be able to spend time with Brittany until that was finished. So she wanted to make sure she was the very first person Brittany O'Brien met today.

But then Penelope imagined her mom getting in trouble for her missing button.

PENELOPE PICTURED HER MOM'S BOSS EXPLAINING
THAT A MISSING BUTTON IS TOTALLY UNPROFESSIONAL.

Penelope fought the image for fifteen seconds before deciding that she *had* to warn her.

"Mom," she said, pointing to the place where the button wasn't, "you can't possibly go to work like that."

Her mom just smiled and tucked her shirt into her skirt.

"*Voilà!*" she said, and threw out her hands as though the problem was solved. Which it obviously wasn't.

Penelope could still tell there was a button missing. The shirt clearly separated toward the bottom. Besides, it could always come untucked during the day, and then everyone would see.

Penelope considered saying this. But her mom was already putting on her lipstick, humming as though nothing was wrong.

Penelope watched her for a moment. She sometimes felt like a totally different species than her mom and Harry. They hardly ever got stressed about anything. They didn't understand Penelope's feelings—not one tiny bit. And both of them had *tons* of friends.

That thought made Penelope even more stressed. She wondered if she had enough time to go into her room and use one of her top-secret calming techniques. Rereading *When We Were Very Young* was usually extremely helpful. Her dad used to read aloud from the book before he left and got a new family. And even though Penelope was (clearly) not very young anymore, she still found the poems lovely and funny.

Drawing pictures or patterns was another excellent calming technique. (Though some of her precious crayons were getting small and stubby from being used over and over. Penelope had to stick a thick sponge under them in her favorite mug so they looked the same height.)

Penelope pulled out her phone to check the time. She was running far too late for a calming technique. If Brittany O'Brien came across Eliza or Alison first, she might get sidetracked and choose the wrong best friend.

The thought was unbearable.

"I've got to go," Penelope told her mom.

"Okay," her mom replied. "And, Poss, please don't worry about me and my shirt. I promise, we'll both be fine."

Penelope shrugged, because sometimes she just had to. Then she kissed her mom good-bye and was very patient during a hug that went for a full five seconds. Immediately after that she rushed downstairs, grabbed her bag, and walked *extremely* fast all the way to school.

The school grounds were deserted except for one lone figure on the basketball court.

"Penny! Penny! Over here!"

Oscar Finley held up a basketball in the palm of one hand. The other hand was rolled up and pressed to his lips like a megaphone.

"Penny!" he repeated.

Penelope marched across the basketball court. Oscar Finley was one of those kids who just seemed to pop up everywhere. And wherever he popped up, he did something to get on Penelope's nerves. If Brittany O'Brien arrived at school right this moment, she might actually think Penelope's name was Penny!

She had asked Oscar several times not to shorten her name, but it seemed she would have to ask him again. Clearly, Oscar Finley was a slow learner.

As Penelope marched, she felt the good, sensible, calm Penelope being taken over by the bossy, angry, frustrated one.

She was going to give Oscar a very good

talking-to. But as she walked, Penelope recalled that Oscar Finley had voted for her to be Class Captain. He told her he'd voted for her. Ms. Pike hadn't revealed the actual vote count, but Penelope (who was very good at figuring things out) suspected she had received only two votes—hers and Oscar's. Everyone else would have voted for Eliza Chung.

By the time she reached Oscar, Penelope had calmed down.

"Oscar," she said patiently, "please can you remember to call me by my full name?"

"Sure," Oscar said. He didn't seem to understand how serious she was, but Penelope didn't have time to comment. Oscar seemed to be all around her at once, dribbling the ball and switching it from hand to hand.

"Defend me," he urged, "then I'll try to make a fast break."

Penelope wasn't certain she knew *how* to defend, but she supposed she could do this favor for Oscar. The basketball court was a good place to keep an eye out for Brittany O'Brien. And besides, it would be good to look busy when Brittany arrived. Penelope stepped in front of Oscar and stuck her hands up in the air.

Oscar circled her, bouncing madly. Penelope turned with him.

"Good defense," Oscar said, "but now I'm breaking free!"

Penelope followed, swatting at the ball as Oscar dribbled toward the net. One of his bounces was so high, the ball hit him in the chin. It then bounced into Penelope's shin, but she absolutely failed to grab it. Oscar didn't even seem to notice. When he got the ball back and took his shot, it only reached halfway to the rim before falling back to the court and rolling away. Oscar scooped it up and ran back to Penelope for another try. Penelope looked around, feeling self-conscious. It would be terribly embarrassing if Brittany O'Brien had arrived in time to see all that clumsiness!

"Try a bit harder, Oscar," she urged, already holding her hands up for a better defense.

Penelope watched out of the corner of her eye as other kids began to arrive. She saw Alison and Eliza, Rita and Tilly. As she defended against Oscar again, doubt knotted in Penelope's stomach. Perhaps she should go and stand with the girls. But sometimes when Penelope tried to join in, the other girls talked and giggled together and didn't seem to hear her. It wouldn't be good if Brittany saw that.

Plus, it looked like Rita was doing most of the talking. She was probably going on about every detail of every boy in her favorite boy band. Once, last semester, Penelope had (only one single time) called the lead singer Hugo instead of Harry, and Rita had made fun of her in front of everyone. Rita still sometimes brought it up. It made Penelope's face burn.

Penelope would absolutely die if that happened in front of Brittany O'Brien.

She could wait outside the classroom, like she did most mornings, so she would be the first in line when Ms. Pike came. But that probably wouldn't look so great to Brittany O'Brien either.

Oscar circled her again, so Penelope decided to concentrate on doing her best defense.

Penelope bit her lip. Class had started *seven* minutes ago. Ms. Pike had finished taking attendance, and still there was no sign of Brittany O'Brien. Penelope squashed down a terrible feeling. What if Brittany had changed her mind about coming to Chelsea Primary?

She glanced around the classroom. Alison was leaning over the table she shared with Eliza, doodling something on Eliza's notebook. Eliza covered her mouth to hide a giggle. Rita Azul was whispering something in Tilly's ear (which was always worrying). Underneath the table, Joanna (the naughtiest girl in the class) was tying her own shoelaces to Sarah's. Normally, Penelope would do something to stop her. In fact, she suspected that was why Ms. Pike had put Joanna at Penelope's table— to teach Joanna how to behave better. But at that moment, with no Brittany O'Brien, she didn't have the heart.

Penelope got out her English work and put her head down. She was decorating the heading with some very careful and complicated coloring when she heard a breathless voice.

"Sorry I'm late, Miss! No joke, my dad got lost about twenty times. It was crazy!"

Penelope looked up. So did the rest of the class. A couple of kids laughed.

Penelope did not gasp. It would not be polite to gasp at her new best friend. Still, seeing Brittany O'Brien was a bit of a shock.

It wasn't her height that was a shock. Brittany O'Brien was only slightly taller than Penelope. It wasn't her nose that was a shock, either. It wasn't pointy, even from the side, but it did have a little ski jump at the end that was a tiny bit similar to Penelope's nose. But her blond hair was definitely not shoulder length. In fact, it was so short around her ears that it must have been cut with an electric clipper. At the top, it stuck up high, a bit like a cockatoo's crest.

Penelope collected her mixed feelings. She breathed them in and breathed them out slowly. Just because Brittany O'Brien had *extremely* short hair and spoke to Ms. Pike in a very casual way—like she was a friend, rather than a teacher—didn't mean that all Penelope's hopes were lost.

"My dad," Brittany O'Brien said with a smile, "can't read a map for nuts. And the GPS was completely messed up, Miss."

Eliza and Alison were both smiling, as though they found Brittany O'Brien very amusing. Penelope sat up very straight and smiled her Very Best and Brightest Smile, hoping Brittany would look her way before she saw Eliza and Alison. Her heart was beating very fast. She took some more deep breaths.

"Don't worry about being late, Brittany,"

Ms. Pike said kindly. "You can call me Ms. Pike. Ms., not Miss."

Brittany nodded. "While we're getting names straight, Ms.," Brittany said quite loudly, as if to make sure the whole class could hear, "I don't go by that name. Not ever. Just call me Bob."

BOB, PENELOPE'S BEST FRIEND?

CHAPTER

3

Penelope frowned. *Bob?* Why would someone with such an elegant name want to go by
their initials instead?

Penelope was examining this thought, and
adding it to Brittany O'Brien's very short hair
and very casual attitude, when she saw Alison
Cromwell put up her hand.

"Ms. Pike?" Alison said. Then she paused
and giggled in a silly way. She pushed Eliza's
books away and Eliza moved to the next

chair. "Can Bob sit with us?" she asked.

Penelope held her breath as Bob sat down between Alison and Eliza. She should have thought of that. But she had been doing too much *examining* to act quickly. That was a big mistake. Once she and Bob became best friends, she would surely be able to help Bob become a Brittany. But right now, Penelope had let a perfectly good chance go by. She was furious with herself.

Penelope tried to get on with her work. But it was difficult to concentrate. Joanna and Sarah were walking, hip to hip, to get a pencil sharpener. And she could see Alison and Eliza in front of her, leaning on their elbows, talking to Bob as though they were already friends. Penelope was so distracted that she made an error on a comprehension question. She had to erase the answer and start all over again.

It seemed as though the morning had stretched out forever when Ms. Pike finally called pencils down.

"Penelope, could you stand up please?" she asked.

Penelope stood behind her chair, pushing it in carefully. She noticed Bob turning around to look at her.

"Bob, this is Penelope Kingston," Ms. Pike said. "Penelope, I wonder if you would show Bob around at recess?"

Bob gave something like a salute, her hand whipping up to her eyebrows. It looked like a very friendly type of salute. Penelope's heart skipped a beat. Ms. Pike was the best, love-liest teacher on the entire planet—possibly even the universe.

"Certainly, Ms. Pike." Penelope made sure her voice was normal and her smile wasn't too big. It wasn't easy. This was definitely the best thing that had happened to her all morning.

As the class packed up, Penelope made a mental list of Things to Show Bob. Obviously, there were practical concerns, like where the girls' bathrooms were. But there were also other important considerations.

Perhaps Bob would like to see the art room, where Penelope's latest painting just happened to be on display? Her painting had been inspired by a Spanish artist, just as the art teacher, Mr. Cattapan, had instructed. Penelope secretly thought her picture was just as good as the original. At least the lady's eyes were in the right spot.

She was just ordering her list from Most Important to Least Important when Oscar interrupted her thinking.

"Hey, Penny-lope, see you at the sausage

sizzle at lunchtime. We're on coleslaw duty. Hopefully, we'll end up with loads of coins to donate. Apparently, the village is getting a well—"

"Thank you, Oscar, I'll be there," Penelope said in her Very Busy voice, turning away from him.

She did not need to be reminded that she'd volunteered to help at the sausage sizzle fundraiser. Helping people less fortunate always made Penelope feel good. Plus, there was an extra bonus. When she helped out at sausage sizzles, Penelope got to make her own sausage, exactly the way she liked it. (With extra coleslaw and a tiny squirt of hot mustard.)

Right now, though, Penelope could not afford to get distracted. Bob had walked straight past Penelope and was heading toward the hallway with Eliza and Alison. She must have forgotten who was showing her around at recess.

Penelope rushed into the hall. Bob had wandered into the area where the boys hung their backpacks. Penelope would have been horrified to make such a mistake. She would be careful to tell Bob very quietly so she wouldn't be embarrassed.

Penelope had to admit she did feel a tiny bit glad that Bob was in the wrong area. For one thing, it meant that Alison and Eliza were finally away from Bob. Also, it gave Penelope a chance to tell her something helpful.

She reached in, avoiding the sea of boys around her, and tapped Bob on the shoulder.

When Bob turned around, Penelope was pleased to note that she was smiling.

"Just to let you know," Penelope said in a very soft voice, "you've actually hung your bag in the—"

"Oh my god! Bob!" Eliza yelled, coming up behind them.

"You're in the boys' area, dude," Alison squealed. "Get. Out. Of. There."

Penelope could not understand why Alison, Eliza, and even Bob were laughing. She did her best to laugh along with them.

"We'd better make sure we show you where the *girls'* bathrooms are," Alison squealed.

PENELOPE PICTURED BOB WALKING INTO THE BOYS' BATHROOM BY ACCIDENT. IT WAS A TERRIBLE IMAGE.

For a moment Penelope forgot she was supposed to be pretending to laugh, but nobody seemed to notice anyway.

"Actually," Penelope said after a few false starts—when she tried to speak but the girls were laughing too much to hear her—"the girls' bathrooms are number one on my list of things to show Bob at recess."

For some reason that set them all off again.

At recess, Penelope led Bob around the school.

"The library is just up those steps, Bob," Penelope said. She pointed and spoke very loudly.

Several girls had (very annoyingly) joined Penelope's tour and were chatting loudly among themselves. Rita and Tilly kept getting left behind and making everyone wait while they caught up. Alison and Eliza were in front of them, and Joanna and Sarah were directly behind.

At least Bob was walking next to Penelope, trying to listen. Joanna kept interrupting. She'd tapped Penelope on the shoulder to interrupt with something random three times already. The last tap had been in the art studio, while Penelope had been telling Bob where the paints and brushes were kept. Bob was probably just about to notice "The Crying Lady"—and possibly even comment on how good it was. That tap had made Penelope very annoyed.

The fourth tap came when they were passing the gym.

"What?!" Penelope said.

SUDDENLY PENELOPE FELT LIKE A KETTLE, JUST WHEN THE WATER WAS ABOUT TO START BOILING.

She breathed deeply to calm herself. "What do you want to say now, Joanna?" Penelope asked.

Joanna wedged herself between Penelope and Bob.

"See that tree?" she said, pointing to a tree with strong branches and a dense canopy of leaves. Bob nodded.

Penelope braced herself. She knew how that tree was used. This was not information to be shared with a student on her very first day.

Especially not Penelope Kingston's Future Best Friend.

Joanna lifted a leafy branch to make a kind of doorway. Penelope and the others waited as Joanna and Bob stuck their heads in.

"If the teachers make you go on a run and you don't want to, you can come in here and hide," Penelope heard Joanna say.

Penelope held her breath. She didn't much like running, and sports were something she was not excellent at, unfortunately. But hiding in the tree was cheating. This was Very Bad Advice.

"Of course, Bob," Penelope said as Bob and Joanna emerged from the tree, "you shouldn't really use that hiding place. If you can't complete a run, you're supposed to tell the teacher."

"Chill, Penelope, it's not a big deal," Eliza chimed in.

Penelope wondered how Eliza ever got to be Class Captain with that attitude.

"Yeah, Penelope, just *relax*," Rita added.

Penelope hated it when people told her to relax (particularly Rita). It had absolutely the opposite effect.

ANGRY THOUGHTS WERE
BOILING AND STEAMING
UP INSIDE PENELOPE.

Truly, she was about to shout them all out.

Right there, in front of Bob.

WHICH WAS WHY IT WAS
ESPECIALLY GOOD TIMING
WHEN THE BELL RANG.

CHAPTER

After recess, Penelope finished a math work sheet, then finished coloring in the heading of her English assignment.

Then Ms. Pike kicked off reading time by asking everyone to bring in their favorite books to share on Friday morning. She wrote a reminder on the board, too, so the students wouldn't forget.

Please bring your favorite book to share.

Penelope instantly knew what she would bring: *When We Were Very Young*. In fact, she was quite excited to be able to share her favorite book, and wondered what the other kids would bring. But she didn't say anything aloud. In Ms. Pike's class, reading time was silent time. *Nobody* talked. Even Joanna (the naughtiest girl in the class) was well behaved. That was one of the good things about Ms. Pike. Most of the time, she was not a strict teacher. But when she said, "No talking," everyone knew she was serious.

The only problem with silent time was that it meant Penelope couldn't communicate with Bob. She wanted to suggest that Bob wait for her while she worked at the sausage sizzle at lunchtime. Then they could take the tour again, just the two of them this time.

Unfortunately, Bob was still sitting between Eliza and Alison, so they had first dibs on speaking to her when silent time was finished.

"Let's quickly eat a sausage, and then we can

play dodgeball," Penelope heard Eliza suggest. It was not a good feeling when Bob agreed right away, sounding very enthusiastic. In fact, it made Penelope feel helpless (which was one of her absolutely least favorite feelings). It was as though all her nerve endings wanted to act immediately to change what was happening, but she couldn't think of a single thing to say or do that would actually work. Which meant the nerve endings were kind of bouncing with absolutely nowhere to go. Dodgeball wasn't the sort of game you could join halfway through. By the time Penelope had finished working at the sausage sizzle, she would have lost her chance to spend any time with Bob. After the disappointing events of recess, that was unthinkable.

But Penelope wasn't a fan of the game, so she had a hard decision to make. And she needed to make it very quickly.

Penelope was never very good at dodging. Today she was even worse. Penelope couldn't stop thinking about Oscar's face when she told him she wasn't going to help out at the sausage sizzle. She could have handled it if Oscar was angry with her. In fact, that was the reaction she'd been hoping for. If Oscar got angry, Penelope could get angry right back at him. After all, she hadn't given him a proper reason for pulling out. For all Oscar knew, Penelope could be feeling extremely ill.

BUT NOW THAT PENELOPE HAD THOUGHT ABOUT IT, OSCAR HADN'T LOOKED ANGRY. HE'D LOOKED DISAPPOINTED.

Just as she was thinking about Oscar's dis-appointed face, Tilly pushed her. Okay, Tilly was actually pushing her out of the way of the oncoming ball. But Penelope had already slipped twice by herself. And she did not like to be pushed. Just as she was struggling to control her anger, the ball thwacked her hard in the thigh.

Penelope grabbed the ball and held it against her so no one could get it. She could feel her leg throbbing.

There were words coiled down deep inside her. All the stress of the morning and all the things that had gone wrong with Project Best Friend had wound them up tight. Now they flew out of her mouth like a scary jack-in-the-box when the music stops.

"THIS IS THE MOST STUPID GAME IN THE ENTIRE WORLD! I CAN'T BELIEVE YOU GIRLS WANT TO PLAY

SOMETHING SO ABSOLUTELY LAME AND RIDICULOUS."

She looked at the girls, her eyes blazing. It was hard to focus through blazing eyes, but it looked as if everyone was frozen to the spot. Bob started hopping around, stretching one leg at a time, but other than that, everyone was still. Still enough for Penelope to notice the mud on their legs and dresses. The mud on Penelope's thigh had dried a little. She flicked it off with her free hand.

"AND NOW YOU'RE GOING TO TRACK MUD ALL THROUGH OUR CLASSROOM."

She threw the ball to the ground and stormed off.

Penelope sat in her favorite booth in the library, by the window, and rubbed her thigh. It wasn't throbbing anymore. There would probably be a bruise, but the throbbing inside her head was way, way worse.

What she had done would not disappear like a bruise.

Bob hadn't even known her for a whole day. She hadn't got to know the good, sensible, and calm Penelope before meeting the bossy, angry, frustrated Penelope. Who no one could possibly want for a best friend.

Through the window, Penelope could see the girls. She could also see the courtyard, where the last remnants of the sausage sizzle were being packed up. But both sights were hazy because tears were welling in Penelope's eyes. This was Truly Terrible. Crying in public was the second worst thing you could do. It was bad enough that she'd gone and done the *very* worst thing by having an outburst in front of everyone. The library booth was fairly private, but if

Penelope didn't get her tears under control, she would end up with red eyes and blotchy skin, which would be extremely telltale. Bob would probably think she was an absolute mess.

Penelope squeezed her eyes shut and forced herself to think of kittens. Although she'd never had a kitten, she did have a kitten calendar at home. She conjured up an image of the white fluffy one with the pink bow. This particular kitten (from October) had helped her out several times before. Thankfully, it was working now, too.

Penelope wiped away the tears on her cheek. Although she had managed to stop crying, she was too upset to eat. Her tummy didn't know that yet, though. Its rumble sounded like thunder. Which was appropriate, in a way, since she felt as if a storm was going on inside her.

The rumble gave way to a thud. For a moment, Penelope thought the thud might be part of the storm. But when it came again, she realized that pieces of bark were being thrown against the window.

It was Oscar. He had a sausage in a bun in one hand. With the other, he was beckoning to Penelope to come down.

Oscar smelled like a barbecue. He smelled of sausages and onions and donations for very good causes.

"I saved this for you," he said, handing Penelope the sausage. Penelope didn't say anything. After the last few things that had come out of her mouth, she wasn't sure speaking was a good idea. Instead, she took a bite of the sausage. Oscar had made it exactly the way she liked it, with extra coleslaw and a tiny squirt of hot mustard.

Penelope finished her mouthful. "I'm sorry Oscar," she said very softly. "I'm so sorry for not doing the sausage sizzle with you. It was a bad decision."

Oscar shrugged. A curl of hair flopped down over his forehead.

"Don't look so sad. It doesn't matter," he said. "I got one of the older girls to help."

Penelope managed a small smile. The older girls were always going on about how cute Oscar was. Personally, Penelope couldn't see it. But suddenly she realized that the *inside* of Oscar Finley was very, very nice.

"Penny, I don't know what happened today," Oscar said.

Penelope was on the verge of correcting him when she stopped herself. She wanted to hear what Oscar had to say—even more than she wanted him to call her Penelope.

"It's very weird for you to bail like that. You've helped with practically every fund-raiser the Parents Committee has come up with. You've done even more than I have. I checked with Gwen."

Penelope tilted her head to the side. Gwen had been on the Parents Committee ever since Penelope first started school. Which was a little strange, since her kids had finished primary school years ago. But Gwen was very nice and very dedicated. Penelope had a sneaking suspicion that she stayed on the committee because it made her feel needed.

THEN PENELOPE REMEMBERED OSCAR'S FACE AS HE HAD PASSED HER THE PERFECT SAUSAGE.

"So you're not angry with me?" she asked.

All the clues suggested that he wasn't, but Penelope wanted to be extra sure. Being extra sure would make it slightly easier to go back into the classroom after her outburst.

"Nope," Oscar said. His mouth stretched into a wide grin. "I figure you deserve a second chance. But just so you know, I signed you up for the next three fund-raisers."

Penelope smiled back.

Usually she found it annoying the way Oscar popped up everywhere. But she was very, very glad he'd popped up now.

CHAPTER

5

Penelope was already at her table when the other girls came in from lunch. Oscar had walked in with her, but now he was at his own table, all the way across the room. For some reason, that seemed much farther away than usual.

Penelope made a very big effort to sit up straight. Probably the best thing would be if everyone tried to forget what had happened. She even attempted a smile as Eliza and Rita walked through the door.

But her smile was not returned. In fact, although it was hard to be sure, Penelope thought she saw Rita roll her eyes. Which would have been very rude.

Penelope definitely felt bad about her explosion. She wished that, if she'd had to explode, it could at least have been about something important. Like the girls taking over her tour of the school. If that had happened, though, things would probably be even worse right now.

She kept smiling as Bob entered the classroom with Joanna.

PENELOPE'S SMILE FELT LIKE IT WAS STITCHED ON.

But she didn't get a chance to see Bob's expression, because Ms. Pike spotted them.

"You girls look like you've taken a tumble or two," she said. "Perhaps you could step outside and brush yourselves off before you spread half the running track in here?"

Joanna giggled. She turned to face Penelope and cupped her hand over the side of her mouth so Ms. Pike couldn't see. But Penelope definitely saw. Joanna stuck her tongue out at Penelope, then headed out of the classroom.

Joanna stuck her tongue out quite frequently. In fact, tongue sticking was something Joanna seemed quite passionate about. She had several different versions, from making a point at the end to a whole rolled tongue. It was disgusting, but Penelope had almost become used to it. Almost.

This time it bothered Penelope a lot.

Penelope looked at the clock above Ms. Pike's desk. There were still ninety-three minutes of class to get through. She pressed her lips together to get rid of the wobble. Then she got on with her work.

For the rest of the day, Penelope worked hard and didn't talk to anyone. Occasionally, she found herself staring at Bob's back. In fact, Penelope could tell anyone, if they asked, how many freckles were on Bob's neck. She could also tell Ms. Pike that Bob was wearing a chain around her neck (if she wanted to, which she didn't—even though it was against school rules).

Bob's chain made Penelope think of some of the charms she'd made. And that it might be better to give Bob the frog or perhaps the mini-bicycle instead of earrings, since Bob didn't have her ears pierced. Penelope let out a sigh. It seemed that giving Bob her best friend gift (absolutely free) was a long way off. Perhaps it would never, ever happen.

It also seemed (from the back, at least) as though Bob was getting along well with Eliza and Alison. Penelope could see that Alison, in particular, was being very chatty. When Alison talked she often moved her head from side to side. It was very hard to watch, and Penelope took far too long to complete the book quiz Ms. Pike had given them. She came second to Felix Unger, a boy who sat at Oscar's table. Felix Unger was the best basketball player in the whole grade. He was good at English, too, but not normally good enough to beat Penelope.

After the final bell rang, Penelope waited for everyone to leave the classroom before packing up her things. In the hallway, past the lockers,

Oscar was standing with Felix Unger, a basket-ball in his arms. Felix had one foot out the door, as though he was desperate to get out on the court. But Oscar was holding his arm. Penelope suddenly realized that Oscar was making Felix wait for her.

Oscar narrowed his eyes, looking at Penelope in a concerned way. He seemed to be checking that she was okay.

"I'm going to go and shoot a few hoops with the Unger," he said. "You know, give him a few tips on how it's done."

Despite the terrible day she'd had, Penelope felt a little smile creep onto her lips. A smile that wasn't stitched on.

"Wanna come, Penny?" he asked.

Penelope shook her head. Felix immediately ran off, but Oscar lingered for a second. A sec-ond was all Penelope needed.

"I have things I need to do. But thanks for asking, Oscar Finley," she whispered in his ear.

As Penelope walked toward the school gate, she looked over at the basketball court. Felix was pointing at a spot on the backboard, clearly telling Oscar where to aim.

Oscar's first shot fell short. So did his second. But the third shot went in, not even touching the sides of the rim. Without planning to, Penelope clapped. Oscar must have heard, because he turned and gave her a silly bow.

Penelope was very surprised how much watching Oscar try and succeed (and perhaps also that silly bow) puffed out her heart and lifted her spirit.

Yes, there had been a setback in Project Best Friend. Okay, a few setbacks. One part of Penelope felt like the project had totally failed. But another part of her remembered that people who strive for excellence do not give up easily.

Cell phones were not allowed in school, but as soon as she left the school grounds, Penelope pulled out her phone, switched it on, and texted Grandpa George.

> I started the project today, but it's not going very well. In fact, it's going very badly. What should I do? Love, me.
>
> P.S. Is it possible to switch star signs? Sometimes I don't like being a Gemini. :(

CHAPTER

6

Penelope kept her phone in her hand as she walked home, waiting for a response. She stopped outside her favorite house and sighed deeply. Recently, a FOR SALE sign had appeared in the front yard. Penelope had taken a photo of the sign and sent it to her dad, just in case he wanted to buy the house. Unfortunately, he did not.

The house was painted white, with a huge bay window upstairs that made Penelope think of princesses and very long hair.

MORE THAN ONCE PENELOPE HAD FANTASIZED ABOUT LIVING IN THE FRESHLY PAINTED, ELEGANT HOUSE.

The FOR SALE sign had been there for a couple of weeks. But today there was a sticker on the sign that said SOLD.

Penelope started to walk faster. Honestly, some days it was extremely difficult to hold on to her hopes.

Penelope's phone rang just as she was walking past the park. A picture of Grandpa George, with his big smile and his gray speckled handlebar mustache, appeared on the screen. There were some children over in the gazebo, but both the swings were empty, so Penelope went over and sat down.

"Sorry, darling," Grandpa George said. "I just got your text. I've been in my dream analysis group."

Penelope heard him say good-bye to his old friend Fred. Grandpa had once told her Fred dreamed almost every night that he was flying. The only thing that changed was the scenery below him. Fred said it was like traveling the world without ever having to buy a plane ticket. It seemed very lovely and funny to Penelope, and made her like Fred very much.

"Tell Fred happy travels from me," Penelope said. She waited a moment while Grandpa delivered the message.

"Fred says you're a treasure," he relayed. "And I'll second that."

Penelope smiled, but her smile was small. It

was good to know that Grandpa and his friends thought she was a treasure, but most girls had people their own age who thought they were great.

"Sweetheart," Grandpa said, "you can't change your star sign. But there are many good things about being a Gemini. Are you having an existential crisis?"

Penelope had never heard the word "existential" before. She had no idea what it meant. But that often happened with Grandpa, so Penelope had learned to make a good guess based on the words she did know. And she definitely knew what a crisis was.

Penelope let her legs dangle under the swing while she told Grandpa what had happened. She left out certain bits. For instance, she didn't tell him about Project Best Friend because it would be too embarrassing to admit (even to Grandpa

George) that she had to work so terribly hard just to make one single best friend. But she did tell him about Bob and the tour and the outburst.

Grandpa George was an excellent listener. It wasn't just that he listened to the words she was saying. It was the way he listened *between* the words.

"Darling, can you hold on a moment?" he said when Penelope had finished. "I'm just going to check your chart."

While she waited, Penelope pushed off with her feet and started swinging. She could hear the rustle of papers as Grandpa George went through her charts. There was no telling how long he would be.

When Penelope looked up again, there was a little girl standing in front of her. She was wearing a frilly T-shirt and a denim dress. Her fine hair was in a loose topknot.

Penelope supposed she was about three years old. Her half sister, Sienna, was three years, two months, and eight days old, so Penelope was basing her guess on that.

"Can you push me?" the little girl said, pointing at the empty swing next to Penelope.

Penelope nodded, but before the little girl could climb up, her mother came and whisked her away.

Suddenly, Penelope felt lonelier than ever. She realized she hadn't seen Sienna for a very long time. Penelope was very glad when her grandpa came back on the phone.

"All right, my love," Grandpa George said. "There's some indication here that you've been swimming upstream."

"Grandpa, I haven't been swimming at all," Penelope said, confused.

Grandpa George laughed. "What that means, love," he said, "is that maybe you've been trying too hard. All indicators on your chart say the best thing right now is to go with the flow."

Penelope walked home considering what Grandpa had said. She thought she might even discuss the matter with her mom. But when she got home, her mom and Harry were on the couch, glued to a TV show where people dare each other to do strange and dangerous things. They were laughing uproariously (though honestly, Penelope had no idea why), and Penelope didn't want to interrupt.

Alone in her bedroom, Penelope sat at her lovely white desk drawing sketches of jewelry she would like to make in the future. It was a very calming activity—even though some of her crayons were stubby. While some of Penelope's brain was busy with Creative Ideas, another part now felt free to think about Grandpa's suggestion.

The idea of going with the flow seemed very difficult. She was used to trying exceptionally hard and getting excellent results. She wasn't the type to just let things happen. But Grandpa George's charts were (mostly) accurate, and filled with very good suggestions.

As she finished a sketch of a bow tie with polka dots that would most likely become a terrific button, Penelope felt that she could actually do this thing.

Tomorrow she would just have to try exceptionally hard to not try at all. She was going to go with the flow.

The next morning, Penelope woke at the usual time to the soothing strums of her harp alarm.

She was quite surprised when she peeked into Harry's room and saw that he was already gone, most likely on his way to soccer practice. The second surprise was her mom's clunky footsteps coming down the hall.

Suddenly the idea of being woken by her mom seemed very appealing (even though it wasn't really being woken, since she was already awake), so Penelope jumped back into bed and pulled the covers over her head.

"Morning, Poss," her mom said, peeling the covers down to Penelope's chin. "You slept through your alarm. Are you okay?"

Penelope frowned. Now that it was morning, she felt anxious all over again. If the girls were still angry with her, today would be absolutely horrible, too. Her confidence from last night had faded. Suddenly, she wasn't sure she'd be any good at going with the flow. And besides, what if she did manage to go with the flow and Bob noticed her less, not more?

Penelope had heard that some kids occasionally had a day off from school even if they weren't actually sick. Perhaps it was because they had a problem and could think of a better solution from home. She decided to mention this fact to her mom.

"Honey, if you want to take the day off, that's okay," her mom replied. "It's not like you do it all the time. Maybe you could treat yourself. Stay in bed or watch TV."

Penelope noticed her mom looking at her watch. "Mom," she said, "are you late for something?"

Penelope's mom slowly rubbed her hands together. "The big boss is holding a meeting for all staff at seven forty-five," she said.

Penelope's eyes popped wide open. She quickly checked the time on her phone. Her mom had exactly twelve minutes to make it to work.

PENELOPE IMAGINED HER MOM WALKING IN LATE, WITH THOSE CLUNKY SHOES MAKING SO MUCH NOISE THAT EVERYONE TURNED AND STARED.

"Go!" Penelope said. "I'll be fine."

As her mother left, she snuggled back under the covers and closed her eyes.

PENELOPE IMAGINED A CONVERSATION WITH HER MOM (THOUGH SHE SOUNDED MORE LIKE THE MOTHERS YOU SEE ON TV).

Penelope jumped out of bed and started getting ready for school.

CHAPTER

First thing in the morning was a math test. Penelope felt lucky to be thinking about multiplication and division instead of the other girls being angry with her and going with the flow.

After math class came Penelope's Least Favorite Subject: physical education. There were only two stalls in the girls' bathrooms, so Penelope made sure to get there first so she could get changed in private. Even though she always wore bike shorts under her uniform, like most of the girls, she still had to take off her dress and put on her sports jersey. She was just smoothing down her collar when she heard some of the girls arrive. Through the gap under the stall door, Penelope deduced (by putting together several clues, such as shoe size and sock choice) that the feet belonged to Tilly, Bob, Rita, and Joanna.

"That test was super hard," came Tilly's voice. "I figure I got most of the answers wrong."

Penelope frowned. Tilly often thought she was going to do badly on tests and then did quite well. She almost piped up to remind Tilly of that, but she wasn't sure if that was going with the flow, so she decided not to say anything.

"It was soooo hard," she heard Joanna say.

"Don't you wish, just sometimes, that you had Penelope's brain? You'd get everything right."

Penelope almost said something then. She got excellent results because she worked very hard. As Penelope had told her several times, Joanna was actually extremely smart. She just needed to focus. (Penelope knew this because she had coached Joanna in math after school.) But before Penelope could say anything, Rita spoke.

"Puh-leeze," she said. "Penelope doesn't get *everything* right."

Penelope sat on the toilet seat and lifted her feet up in front of her. Suddenly, it seemed very important that no one knew she was there. Her heart flipped around in her chest like a fish. For a moment, she thought Rita was going to say something humiliating about the Harry/Hugo mistake.

But what she said was worse. "Seriously, she totally cracked up yesterday, right? *This is a silly game. It's absolutely ri-di-cu-lous.*"

Penelope's face was flaming. She hugged her legs and put her head down on her knees. The girls' laughter seemed to go on forever.

"Penelope is the queen of cracking up," Rita continued. "I can think of at least six times when she's lost it. In prep—"

"Gosh, it wasn't *that* bad." Penelope was surprised to hear Bob's voice cutting Rita off. "I mean, Penelope seems very nice. Her school tour was very helpful. And I've definitely had bigger tantrums than her dodgeball one."

Penelope didn't much like the reference to tantrums. She preferred to think of what had happened as an outburst. Still, it was kind of Bob to understand that she was trying her best on the tour (which was difficult with the other girls inter-

rupting and being silly). And it was even kinder of
Bob to stick up for Penelope—especially to Rita.

"Yeah, she's really nice," came Tilly's voice.
"Last week she gave me half her lunch when I forgot mine. And she patted my back when I thought I
was going to throw up after the cross-country run.
She just throws a tantrum every now and then."

"Well," Bob said, and Penelope thought she
could hear a smile in her voice, "out of ten, I'd
give that tantrum a five. I've done way, way
worse. Once I squished a sandwich in a boy's
face because he called me stupid. A jam sandwich. Now *that* was at least a seven."

The girls laughed again. Penelope still didn't
like the word "tantrum," but she was beginning
to feel much, much better.

"Besides," Bob continued, "we all do stuff
like that sometimes."

Rita piped up again. "In second grade, some

kids were messing around and they spilled juice on Penelope's work. She turned bright red and didn't say anything for the rest of the day!"

Penelope wondered if Rita had actually written down a list of all her outbursts over the years, or if she'd stored them all up in her head.

"That's actually so true, Bob," Tilly said. Penelope was pleased that Tilly was ignoring Rita's comment. "Like, for instance, you have a bad temper too, don't you, Jo? Remember when you screamed your head off at the boys because they won that basketball game?"

"Yeah, and when you're mad you start crying, Tilly," Joanna replied. "You bawled your eyes out that time Felix knocked your arm and you dropped your pink doughnut in the dirt!"

"I just have overactive tear ducts," said Tilly, but she sounded amused rather than angry. "Anyway, that was *years* ago."

"It was *last* year," Joanna replied with a giggle. "Boohoo."

"See?" Bob said. "What Penelope did wasn't a big deal."

"Right," came Tilly's voice.

"Penelope also had a major meltdown in . . ." Rita's voice trailed off as the others all agreed with Bob.

"Yeah, of course it wasn't," Joanna said.

"It so wasn't last year, Joanna," Tilly continued. "And stop sticking your tongue out. It's disgusting."

Penelope could hear Joanna's giggle getting smaller and smaller as the girls left the bathrooms. She snuck a peek under the door to check that there was no one still there. Then she left the stall and fixed her ponytail in front of the mirror, smiling at her reflection. Bob was absolutely going to be the greatest Best Friend in the whole world.

All she had to do now was to keep following Grandpa George's advice.

As Penelope had expected, going with the flow was very difficult. At recess, she found herself sitting at the benches in the courtyard (frying in the hot sun) rather than under the shady tree, because most of the other girls (including Bob) were on the benches, too.

Things were back to normal. The girls were so full of chatter that Penelope hardly got a word in. Ordinarily, Penelope would have forced her way into the discussion, even if it was about Rita's boy band or some silly crush Eliza had.

But today, especially after what happened in the girls' bathrooms, Penelope was determined not to force anything.

At lunchtime, going with the flow was almost impossible. Joanna (the naughtiest girl in the class) had brought water balloons to school. She filled them up at the faucet and tossed them randomly at people, which was definitely against school rules.

Penelope stood at the top of the hill and watched. Sarah was the first girl to be water-bombed. She was running away from Joanna, so Penelope could only see her back. But even from a distance, Penelope could see the mark the water made on the back of her dress. Penelope held her breath as she saw Sarah's shoulders shaking, but when Sarah turned around, Penelope realized the shaking was from laughter.

So they were having fun. Nobody was getting hurt. And water was just water. It wouldn't leave a stain.

Penelope remembered to breathe. This was the correct way to think when you were going with the flow. As another water bomb exploded in Alison Cromwell's hair, Penelope didn't even hold her breath. There may have been an extra-long blink, but that was all. And even though the teacher on yard duty, Mr. Joseph, was *supposed* to be aware of what was happening in the playground, but had no idea (just like the day Penelope had earned her Watchful Eye award), Penelope didn't say a word to him.

By the time the school day finished, Penelope had spoken with Bob exactly once.

WHERE IS THE CLOSEST WATER FOUNTAIN?

OVER THERE.

PENELOPE REMEMBERED EXACTLY HOW THAT CONVERSATION HAD GONE.

Even if Bob did think Penelope was nice, and even though she had stuck up for her in the bathroom, Penelope doubted that this conversation could, in any way, be considered the beginning of a very special friendship.

CHAPTER

8

Every Tuesday night (even after her daughter had a rather difficult and very complicated day), Penelope's mother went to Zumba class, so dinner was make-your-own. Penelope looked through the shopping bags on the kitchen counter. She was pretty sure microwave macaroni and cheese wouldn't fulfill the requirements of the food pyramid. But she could put some carrots on the side, though she was almost certain that Harry (who was upstairs on his computer) wouldn't eat them.

Penelope was putting the groceries away and thinking about her very complicated day when she felt something oblong and hard underneath the last brown paper shopping bag.

Penelope lifted the bag up. Then she gasped, because what was under the bag was entirely the sort of thing to inspire a gasp. It was a proper gasp, too, where her mouth opened into an O and then she clapped a hand over it.

Right there, on the counter in front of her, was an *entire box* of fifty-two crayons. It was brand-new, still with the plastic covering. On top of the box of fifty-two crayons was a yellow sticky note with her mom's scribbly writing on it.

Hey, Poss,
I hope your day went okay.
Mom x

Penelope clutched the crayons to her chest where she was quite sure her heart was. The box felt cool against her school dress.

A little tear blurred her vision for a moment, but not because she was sad.

On Wednesday morning, before her mom got up, Penelope slipped a very lovely and very crayon-colorful picture under her door.

★ ★ ★

Wednesday went pretty much the same way Tuesday had. So did Thursday. There always seemed to be a crowd around Bob, and Penelope hardly got a chance to talk to her. Penelope was seriously beginning to wonder if going with the flow was going to work.

It was a relief to stay back after school on Thursday to help Ms. Pike prepare for their monthly session at the senior center down the road. Penelope loved going there. Sometimes the children would sing a song. Other times, someone would recite a poem.

At the last performance, Joanna had, unexpectedly, done a very nice job with "The Man from Snowy River," which had made two of the elderly folk tear up.

For their visit on Friday afternoon, the class

was going to perform a lovely, bright song that Mrs. Raven, the music teacher, had taught them called "Love and Marriage." Penelope had noticed that Bob was a quick learner. She knew all the words already, even though she'd missed most of the rehearsals.

Penelope suspected that some of the boys (not Oscar) were *deliberately* forgetting the lyrics. She had suggested a solution to Ms. Pike, and was now writing the lyrics, very clearly, on a large piece of cardboard so there could be no excuse.

It was very pleasant sitting in the classroom alone with Ms. Pike. Ms. Pike's voice was lovely as she dictated the words. Penelope particularly liked the line, "They go together like a horse and carriage." She liked the idea of things going together so neatly.

Penelope couldn't help worrying about who she would end up partnering with on the way to the senior center. Going with the flow was taking an exceptionally long time to work, so it clearly wouldn't be with Bob. If it had to be a boy (which had happened before), she hoped it would be Oscar. But with each moment she spent with Ms. Pike, Penelope felt calmer and more settled.

Walking home afterward, Penelope still had a bit of the calm feeling inside her. As she passed her favorite house, she paused. There was a big truck in the driveway. Two muscly men were tilting a couch, trying to fit it through the front door.

Penelope sighed. Obviously, her dream of living in the house was over. She looked up at the open bay window.

INSTEAD OF A LONG-HAIRED PRINCESS, PENELOPE SAW A REGULAR GIRL WITH EXTREMELY SHORT HAIR.

"Penelope! Come in!" Bob yelled, waving down at her.

CHAPTER

9

Penelope stood in the driveway, her heart racing. Maybe it was because it was such a big change from feeling so calm, but she felt as though a panicked horse had lost its way and was galloping wildly inside her chest.

At last, this was an opportunity to spend some time with Bob. But it was entirely unexpected. Penelope was not prepared. She would have to think up a conversation topic on the spot.

THE ONLY THING THAT JUMPED INTO PENELOPE'S MIND WAS THAT SHE COULD (FINALLY) SHOW BOB HER VIDEO.

She could also try to explain that the way she'd acted after her leg got thwacked in dodgeball was how anyone would have acted, and that it was a very rare *outburst* (and definitely not a tantrum). But she suspected that wasn't an actual topic of conversation.

Penelope took one of her biggest ever extremely deep breaths. *I'm going with the flow,* she chanted inside her head, a little bit for herself and a little bit for her grandpa, who could (sometimes) pick up on Penelope's thought waves. She pulled out her phone and quickly texted her mom to say she would be late home, adding an X at the end.

"Sure," she called up to Bob, very casually. "I'm coming in." But Bob wasn't at the window anymore.

Penelope stepped cautiously inside the open door.

The house was as elegant on the inside as it was on the outside. Even the fact that there were boxes all over the place and no furniture in the foyer couldn't hide it. The ceilings were so high, they made Penelope feel even smaller than usual.

Bob was standing at the bottom of some very grand stairs. Behind her was a man with a big smile and heavy glasses.

"Dad, this is Penelope," Bob introduced her.

Bob's dad extended his hand and lowered his head as though Penelope was an important guest. "I'm very pleased to meet you," he said.

Penelope felt funny as she shook his hand. It was always a bit odd meeting fathers who actually lived with their kids. Some of them were not at all nice or polite, so they didn't affect her much. But when they *were* nice and polite, like Bob's father, something seemed to tickle (or maybe scratch) Penelope's heart in an uncomfortable way.

Luckily, Bob didn't seem to notice the tickling or scratching.

"Come and see my room," she said, stomping barefoot up the stairs without waiting for Penelope to answer. "It's awesome. Kind of like a fairy-tale bedroom. It feels like Rapunzel might have hung out there once upon a time."

Penelope felt a smile playing around her lips.

As they arrived at her bedroom door, Bob grinned and threw up her hands at the same time, as though she was happy with her new room but also in despair at the state of it. Penelope peeked inside. There was a bed in the center of the room, but that was all. Nothing was unpacked. Twelve rather large boxes were stacked in the corner.

Bob shrugged. "It's going to take fifteen forevers to get my stuff sorted out," she said.

Penelope tilted her head. She wasn't fond of sayings that didn't make sense. A while ago, Oscar had said he was going to put 110 percent into a school assignment. Penelope had pointed out how silly that was. (Now, since the sausage incident, she kind of wished she hadn't.)

Penelope let Bob's "fifteen forevers" go without comment.

Getting sorted out was something she excelled at, and it would not take her even one forever to do it.

"Would you like me to help?" she asked.

"Seriously, Penelope, you are a legend! I could never have made my own room look this awesome on my own!"

Penelope smiled. Bob's bedroom was coming along nicely. Her clothes were color coded, which was important, since the clothes rack was exposed.

Bob's personal knickknacks were all out on display, including an interesting array of plastic molded animals. Penelope had arranged them carefully on the shelf in front of the bay window, making sure that no predator was close to its prey.

As well as making the room look great,

Penelope had also found out many things about Bob. She now knew, for instance, that Bob's mother had a Very Big Job and that the family had moved several times because of it. She knew this was the first house Bob's family had ever owned, and that this was because Bob's mother had landed the Very Biggest Job, so (hopefully) they would not have to move again.

She also knew that Bob was feeling quite frustrated (and Penelope could definitely relate to this) because she couldn't find her collection of books. She would have to hunt *forever* if she was going to bring her favorite book to class the next day. (Penelope offered to lend Bob one of hers, but Bob said thanks for the offer, but that it wouldn't be right.)

So far, Bob didn't know much about Penelope, though. It had been so nice working on the bedroom and listening to Bob chatting away that Penelope had quite forgotten, even about the video on her phone.

Penelope opened the second-last box and pulled out a print. It was a painting of a bridge over a pond covered in lilies. It was quite a nice painting, although secretly Penelope thought it might be better if it was a little less fuzzy.

"Do you want it here?" she asked Bob, indicating some bare wall space.

Bob shook her head. "Not there," she said. "That space is reserved."

"What for?" Penelope asked.

Bob's grin was contagious, even though Penelope wasn't sure why she was grinning.

"I'll show you," Bob said.

The next thing Penelope knew, Bob was doing a handstand against the wall. She was a bit worried, since the walls were white and Bob's bare feet looked a little grubby, but she decided not to say anything. It was Bob's room, after all.

"Come on! Go next to me!" Bob's upside-down voice was squeaky.

Penelope bit her lip as she took off her shoes. So far, going with the flow had been a good idea—this afternoon, at least. She couldn't ruin it now.

Although she hadn't done a handstand in some time, Penelope found it pretty easy. In fact, her arms felt very strong. Her hair almost touched the floor. Bob's, on the other hand, remained exactly as it looked the right way up. Her face, though, was bright red as she turned it toward Penelope.

"This is very relaxing, right?" Bob said. "Sometimes I do this to get calm. Different thoughts come into my head upside down. Like, right now, I'm realizing that I've been talking too much and you know loads about me, but I hardly know anything about you. So . . ."

The "so" was said with a little movement of her head to indicate that Penelope should talk now. Penelope's blood seemed to tingle in her head.

"Well, I have some techniques I use to calm down, too," Penelope admitted. "Though they're not handstands." She took her voice down a notch. Penelope had never actually shared her top-secret calming techniques with anyone, but now seemed quite a good time to do it.

"I like to read or draw when I want to calm down," she said.

"Cool," Bob said. "Both those things are totally calming. What else?"

Bob's response made Penelope feel very pleased. She wanted to continue the conversation about calming techniques, but it seemed more important to explain something else first.

"One thing I'd like you to know is that I never—well, hardly ever—blow up like I did at dodgeball the other day. It was actually even a surprise to me. Normally, I am quite good at being calm and sensible."

Saying she was normally quite good at being sensible while she was upside down seemed a little bit strange.

It must have seemed funny to Bob, too, because she giggled.

"Sometimes," Penelope tried again, "not very often, but just occasionally . . ."

Penelope sighed. It was a difficult thing to explain, and even if she did manage to explain it, what if Bob thought she was weird?

"Is it like this?" upside-down Bob asked. "You think you're going to do one thing and you end up totally doing another? Sort of like you've got different people inside you?"

The feeling inside Penelope wasn't just because blood was rushing to her head. Nodding when you're upside down is quite hard to do, and Penelope's hair actually swept the ground when she did it. But Penelope did it anyway. Several times.

Bob blew out a breath before she continued. "That sounded kooky," she giggled. "It's probably not what you were trying to say. I'm not making any sense at all. You probably think I'm nuts."

Penelope found that shaking her head upside down was a bit easier than nodding. At least this time, Bob seemed to notice what she was doing. Penelope could tell she was waiting for her to speak.

"You're *absolutely* not nuts, Bob," Penelope said. "Not to me, anyway. What you said makes perfect sense."

CHAPTER

"Well, well, well," Bob's dad said, standing in the doorway and looking around Bob's bedroom. "You girls have done an amazing job in here."

Penelope quickly got out of her handstand and stood up.

Bob stayed put.

"I think banana smoothies are in order," Bob's dad continued. "In fact, I've already made them. They're in the kitchen."

Now Bob was very quick to get out of her handstand.

"Thanks, Dad!" she said as she zoomed across the room.

As they crossed paths, Bob's dad leaned down and kissed Bob on the top of the head.

Of course, Penelope's dad kissed her hello and good-bye when she visited. Sometimes he even kissed her good night when she slept over. It seemed to Penelope, though, that this kiss was for absolutely no reason. Bob and her dad didn't even seem to notice it had happened. They acted as if those sorts of random kisses were totally normal.

Bob and her dad both walked out of the bedroom. But the tickly, scratchy thing in Penelope's heart made her freeze for a second.

Suddenly, Penelope imagined her own dad delivering a random kiss like that. . . .

...ONTO SIENNA'S HEAD.

Bob peeked around the doorway. "Are you coming or what?"

The banana smoothie was so thick that the girls had to work hard to get it up the straws. Bob crossed her eyes as she sucked. She looked so funny that Penelope completely forgot about her dad and Sienna and random kisses. She giggled so much that her smoothie (which she'd managed to get three-quarters of the way up her straw) was slowly going backward.

"I give up!" Bob said.

She took the straw out of her drink and went to get some spoons. Penelope followed. On the way back, she noticed a framed photo sitting on the counter.

"Who's that?" Penelope asked, instantly thinking of Sienna again. Bob picked up the photo.

"That's my little cousin, Lincoln," she said, taking the photo back to the barstool with her. Both girls took a spoonful of smoothie (which Penelope now discovered was very delicious, even though it was more like food than a drink).

"He's very cute," Penelope said.

This was true. Lincoln, who looked to Penelope to be about three years old, had soft blond curls and big blue eyes. He looked like one of the cherubs Penelope had seen on count-less cards and paintings.

"He might *look* cute, but he's a rat," Bob said.

Penelope could not help grinning. She prob-ably shouldn't encourage Bob to talk like that, but she could not stop smiling. As soon as Bob mentioned a rat, Penelope found herself men-tally adding whiskers to the photo of Lincoln.

"I'll give you the perfect example," Bob con-tinued. "My auntie put him on my lap. I didn't mind that, even though he had a huge gob of snot hanging out of his nose. Then he started leaning right into my face. My auntie was going on about how cute it was that he wanted to kiss me, so I thought I'd just get it over and done with, snot and all. Then the little rat *BIT* me, right on the nose!" Bob pinched her nose to indicate where the little rat had bitten her.

Something about the way Bob told the story

struck Penelope as hilarious. It was almost as though Bob had her very own special language. With a flash, Penelope realized that she completely understood why Bob didn't want to be called Brittany. The name (as much as Penelope loved it) didn't suit her one bit.

Penelope couldn't remember the last time she'd laughed so hard. And she didn't think there had *EVER* been a time someone else had been laughing along with her.

When their laughter had finally been reduced to giggles, Penelope got out her phone.

"Oh my god, you've got an iPhone!" Bob squealed. Then she cupped a hand to her mouth and yelled loudly up the stairs, "Dad! Penelope has an iPhone!"

It was a moment before her dad's voice boomed back. "Tell her congratulations."

Bob rolled her eyes. "I'll *never* get a phone,"

she said. "But give me your number anyway."

It was very exciting watching Bob write her name and phone number on a magnetic board on the fridge. It was almost like a promise that Bob really planned to stay in close contact with Penelope! Penelope was also thrilled to note that Bob had very neat handwriting, just like hers.

In fact, there were quite a few things (though maybe not the things she'd originally hoped for) that she and Bob had in common.

After Penelope added Bob's number to her phone, she scrolled through the photos until she came to one of Sienna.

"This is my half sister," she said, showing Bob the photo.

"She's also very cute," Bob said. "She looks very sweet, too. I bet she wouldn't pretend to kiss you and then bite your nose."

"She is very cute," Penelope agreed.

The photo showed Sienna, all big brown eyes and chubby cheeks, wearing her tiara (the best piece of jewelry Penelope had ever made), along with a fairy costume, and holding a wand. Penelope had taken the photo during the last school vacation, when she and Harry had stayed with her dad for a few days.

"But sometimes she's not very sweet," Penelope continued. "You know what she did with that wand?"

Bob shook her head.

"She told me to close my eyes while she said a fairy spell. Then she thwacked me right over the head with it."

Making Bob totally crack up was one of the best moments in Penelope's Entire Life.

CHAPTER

On the way home from Bob's, Penelope felt extremely excited. It was a bit like the feeling she got when she'd just finished a test and was absolutely sure she'd done well. But today's type of excited was a bit different. For one thing, Penelope tried her very hardest in tests. At Bob's house (and this was very weird), the best moments had been when she'd actually *forgotten* to try. Even though she hadn't even shown Bob her introduction video, she had a lovely feeling that she and Bob were really getting to know each other.

The feeling was very pleasant and satisfying. Penelope was determined to hang on to it.

Later that evening when she was having dinner (and Harry was disgustingly chewing up his noodles and showing her the mush in his mouth), Penelope kept thinking about her and Bob organizing Bob's bedroom together, and Bob calling her a legend.

While she was brushing her teeth (six brushes for each tooth, front and back, and don't forget the gums), she remembered the way they had laughed when they couldn't suck the thick smoothies up their straws.

But when she remembered telling Bob how Sienna had thwacked her over the head, a little air seemed to seep out of her happy memory bubble. Penelope lay straight in her bed, blue teddy bear lying next to her (because he matched the blue flowers on her bedspread), and thought about it.

She had never said anything like that, anything critical, about Sienna before. Well, maybe she'd complained a little to her mom and Harry. But definitely not to anyone outside the family. Until now, she had only told the other girls at school how fabulous it was to have a little half sister. And even though what she'd told Bob was an absolutely true story, part of her felt guilty.

As soon as she started thinking like that, more thoughts jumped in to trample down the happy ones.

There was no doubt that Penelope and Bob had gotten along well. It was starting to seem that they actually had many things in common.

THINGS IN COMMON: Penelope and Bob
- ♥ calming techniques
- ♥ neat handwriting
- ♥ Bob's bedroom reminds us both of princesses
- ♥ little people in our lives who are cute and also naughty
- ♥ smoothies
- ♥ we definitely had a great afternoon together

But that was when they were on their own. Without Alison or Eliza or Tilly or Sarah or Joanna or Rita to compete for Bob's attention.

The truth was, everyone liked Bob.

Bob was popular.

In the end, it didn't really matter whether Penelope tried her very hardest or went with the flow. In the end, Bob would choose who she wanted to be best friends with. And with all the options, the best Penelope supposed she could really, honestly hope for was that Bob would include her as *one* of her friends.

Penelope got up to check that *When We Were Very Young* was safe and ready for the morning in her plaid backpack. Then she climbed back into bed, sighing as she tucked the covers under her chin and drew blue teddy in for a hug. He was probably cold all the way over there by himself.

"Oh well," she whispered comfortingly in his ear, "at least I've got you."

It was quite silly to talk to a teddy bear, and Penelope was definitely going to stop doing it very soon. But blue teddy had been with Penelope for a very long time. He was a very reliable teddy bear. In fact, blue teddy made her think of Oscar, who was always there and always reliable. Penelope found talking to blue teddy and thinking about Oscar strangely comforting. In fact, it relaxed Penelope into a very nice sleep.

At school the next morning, Penelope carefully took *When We Were Very Young* out of her backpack and laid it on the table in front of her. Sarah had brought in her favorite Go Girl book, *Dancing Queen*, and Joanna had a very lovely illustrated copy of *Alice in Wonderland*.

"Let's go around the class, starting from the back," Ms. Pike said. "Felix, can you begin by showing us your book and telling us a few things about it?"

It was lovely to see and hear about everyone's favorite books. There were several Penelope had never even heard of. She smiled as Oscar talked animatedly about *Diary of a Wimpy Kid*. It wasn't her sort of book, but it did sound like it would be fun to read. When Rita's turn came, she held up a book with Harry the pop star's face on the cover. Rita talked about the awesome things she had learned about Harry from reading the book. Penelope didn't think it was all that amazing that Harry enjoyed eating Oreos (most people enjoyed eating Oreos), but she listened politely.

Then came Bob's turn. For a moment, Penelope was concerned that Bob hadn't been able to find her box of books. But then Bob pulled out something she'd had on her lap, under the table. The something was worn and dog-eared and definitely not in peak condition. But it was still the same book as Penelope's own. *When We Were Very Young*.

THINGS IN COMMON: Penelope and Bob
♥ calming techniques
♥ neat handwriting
♥ Bob's bedroom reminds us both of princesses
♥ little people in our lives who are cute and also naughty
♥ smoothies
♥ we definitely had a great afternoon together
♥ favorite book: WHEN WE WERE VERY YOUNG

"I just can't believe we have the same favorite book!"

Even though Bob had said the same sentence three times, Penelope was not at all sick of hearing her say it. She was also delighted to be sitting with Bob under the shady tree, absolutely and totally by themselves.

"My dad used to do the voices aloud." Bob put on a deep voice. "'He went among the villagers and blipped them on the head,'" she said, quoting from one of the poems.

Penelope giggled so much that she ended up lying down and closing her eyes. When she opened them, Rita and Tilly were standing in front of her.

"Why are you way over here?" Rita asked in a grumpy voice. She pointed to the benches in the courtyard. "Come on."

Penelope knew Rita wouldn't have bothered to come and get her if it wasn't for Bob. She waited for Bob to get up and go. But Bob stayed exactly where she was, sitting with her legs crossed. "We'll come over a bit later, Rita," she said. "We're just talking about our fave book."

Rita definitely rolled her eyes. She put her hands on her hips.

"That book," she said, pointing at Bob's dog-eared copy, which lay on the grass next to them (Penelope's was safely in her locker, inside her plaid backpack), "is for babies."

Penelope sat up very straight. Anger bubbled inside her. She was sick of Rita Azul making her feel small and unimportant. She had plenty of things to say about Rita's stupid book, for a start. Penelope was pretty sure there would be a *torrent* of things to say to Rita once she got started.

She looked over at Bob. There was a big frown on Bob's face. It looked very much as though she was (almost) as cross as Penelope.

No one spoke. It was definitely only a matter of seconds before Penelope exploded. She could feel each and every one of the symptoms.

The thudding in her temples, the rush of blood to her face. Penelope felt her mouth open, ready to let loose.

But then Bob moved. As Penelope realized Bob was getting up, the heat of her anger quickly melted away. Suddenly it felt very cold sitting in the shade. Penelope watched, her mouth still open, as Bob stood up. She felt her happiness start to crumple. She'd had her very own friend for such a short time, but it had already changed her life. Going back to the way things had been would make her Unbearably Lonely. Just the thought of it made Penelope's heart ache.

Of course Bob was going to go with Rita. No one wanted to get on the wrong side of Rita Azul. And the other girls over on the benches were waving now.

But the way Bob rubbed her hands together

seemed a bit odd. So did the wink she gave Penelope.

In a heartbeat, Penelope knew what to do. She was not going to explode. That would just give Rita another outburst to add to her list. She stood up next to Bob and rubbed her own hands together. Her blood was still bubbling away inside her, but she ignored it.

Then, right at the same time, the two girls tucked the hems of their uniforms into their bicycle shorts and did a handstand against the tree.

It was lucky that the tree had such a big and sturdy trunk, because very soon everyone was doing handstands against it. There were loads of giggles as the girls timed each other, trying to hold their handstand for the longest time. Bob was absolutely and clearly the winner, but everyone else had fun trying to beat her.

It was Penelope's best recess in a very long time. After a while, even Rita joined in.

Penelope suspected that Rita felt bad about what she'd said. She even told Penelope it was her turn to do the next handstand, when it was actually and obviously Rita's own turn.

When the bell rang for the end of recess, Bob was still upside down.

"Can you wait for me, Penelope?" she said in a whisper. "I need to ask you something."

Penelope nodded. Seeing everyone charge back toward the lockers made her feel a bit edgy. Normally, she would be one of the first to respond to the bell. If you got to the lockers when they were crowded, it took longer to get your books. That could possibly mean being late to class, which would ruin Penelope's Perfect Record for Punctuality.

She'd actually hoped to get there a bit early to let Ms. Pike know (in private) that Penelope would be her partner when they went to the senior center. That way, there wouldn't be any fussing when Ms. Pike called for them to get into pairs.

Still, something inside Penelope told her to stay with Bob. The something was a mixture of Things In Common and funny stories and not-even-trying.

She waited for Bob to come down from her handstand (moving *When We Were Very Young* out of the way just in the nick of time).

"Penelope," Bob said, looking at the ground instead of Penelope (which was quite unusual for Bob), "starting at a new school sucks sometimes."

Except for her very first day at Chelsea Primary, Penelope had never started at a new school. But she could totally imagine how it would suck (although she wouldn't put it that way). It didn't seem at all like it sucked for Bob, though.

"Well, you're doing extremely well," Penelope said encouragingly. "Already everybody likes you."

"Thanks," Bob said, "but everyone goes gaga over you when you're new and different. It happens at every new school I go to. The thing is, it doesn't last that long."

Penelope examined that idea. She doubted that kids would go gaga over her if she started at a new school, but Bob seemed to know what she was talking about.

"I want to get it right this time," Bob continued. "Because it's going to be forever."

Penelope waited. Her heart fluttered.

Bob finally looked up. It was absolutely surprising, but Bob seemed to be feeling shy.

"So, I was just wondering," she said falteringly, "if you would be my partner when we go to visit the oldies this afternoon?"

Penelope felt like she was going to burst with happiness.

Even knowing that they were definitely going to be late for class didn't bother her.

Even Bob calling the elderly folk "the oldies" didn't bother her.

Perhaps the beginning of Project Best Friend had been a disaster. But Penelope had persisted, and her persistence had paid off.

Or perhaps it had been a mixture of persistence and going with the flow. The funniest thing, though, was that the feeling glowing inside Penelope wasn't a feeling of achievement.

As Penelope stood there (being a little late for class) she realized one thing she hadn't really considered at the start of Project Best Friend.

She actually liked Bob. Very, very much. And having a best friend who she liked very, very much was going to be the most amazing thing ever.

Penelope was determined to be the very best Best Friend she could possibly be. After all, best friends didn't come along just every day.

"Actually, Bob," Penelope said, grinning and grinning, "that would be perfect."

132 ★ PENELOPE PERFECT

ABOUT THE AUTHOR

Chrissie Perry is the author of more than thirty books for children and young adults, including thirteen books in the popular Go Girl series and the award-winning *Whisper*. She lives in St. Kilda, Australia, with her husband and three children.

Like Penelope Kingston, Chrissie believes it's great to aim for excellence. But she also has a sneaking suspicion that going with the flow every now and then can also work out just fine.

Penelope is going to camp—

and this year it will be perfect. . . .

Sparkle Spa

Making friends one Sparkly nail at a time!

Did you LOVE reading this book?

Visit the Whyville...

IN THE MIDDLE BOOK HIVE

Where you can:

- Discover great books!
- Meet new friends!
- Read exclusive sneak peeks and more!

Log on to visit now!
bookhive.whyville.net

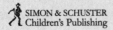